My Pillow and Me

Thank you for
having me come
and read.

Chris Cole

Cover design by Christina Nixon Cole
Book design by Christina Nixon Cole
Illustrated by Hollie Mengert
Production design by Al Morrow

Christina Nixon Cole
Visit my website at www.ladybookpublishing.com
Thank you to Dr. Dan Harper for showing me the light and giving me hope.
And thank you to my best friend, Mici, and my husband Dave.

Printed in the United States of America

First Printing: June 2011

ISBN 978-0615559896

Library of Congress Control Number: 2011960317

Ladybook
publishing

Me and my pillow, my pillow and me.
Oh how comfy, soft,
and snugly!

I take it with me
just about
everywhere.

All over the house.
The bathtub?
No! Not there!

I have to protect it,
as it protects me.
I've got proof.
Look at it!
It's so raggedy.

I take it on car rides, and trips to the store.

But Mom makes me
leave it in the car.
Doesn't she understand
how I want more?

I love my pillow,
my pillow loves me.
Oh how comfy,
soft, and snugly!

I cuddle my pillow,
and pet it and squeeze.
You'll like it, just try it!
Oh, won't you please?

My pillow adores me,
it's by my side wherever I go.

It followed
me to Bud's house,
even after Papa
said, "no"!

I love my pillow,
my pillow loves me.
Oh how comfy,
soft, and snugly!

I've loved my pillow now
for many years.
The thought of
outgrowing it
just brings me to tears.

I see it has holes, rips and tears.
But when I close my eyes, I don't really care.

I took it to Cole's house
to spend the night.
He teased my tattered pillow,
and we had a fight.

Why didn't he understand
how important it is?
If he had a snugly pillow,
I'd respect his.

My pillow has been good to me,
like a best friend.
There to comfort me, cradle me,
and always defend.

I brought it to Granny's
just the other day.

She washed my
raggedy pillow,
while I escaped
to go play.

Now my pillow doesn't stink like a dirty old dog.
But it's still comfy soft, I'm sure I will sleep like a log.

So, now my pillow stays home when I go away.
But I don't miss it, considering how hard I play.

I still love my pillow, my pillow still loves me.
It's so comfy, soft, but now so raggedy!

Night Lights

I'm a big kid now,
my mommy says.
I'm almost ready to say,
so long to those pillow days.

One day I'll go shopping
for a brand new one.
The kind for big kids,
but no doubt, still fun.

Today Dad found a box
for safe keeping.
Knowing it's safe
in the closet
now, that sounds relieving.

I loved my pillow,
my pillow loved me.
It will always be with me
in my memory.

Guess what!

Hurray!

I can't wait for you to see!

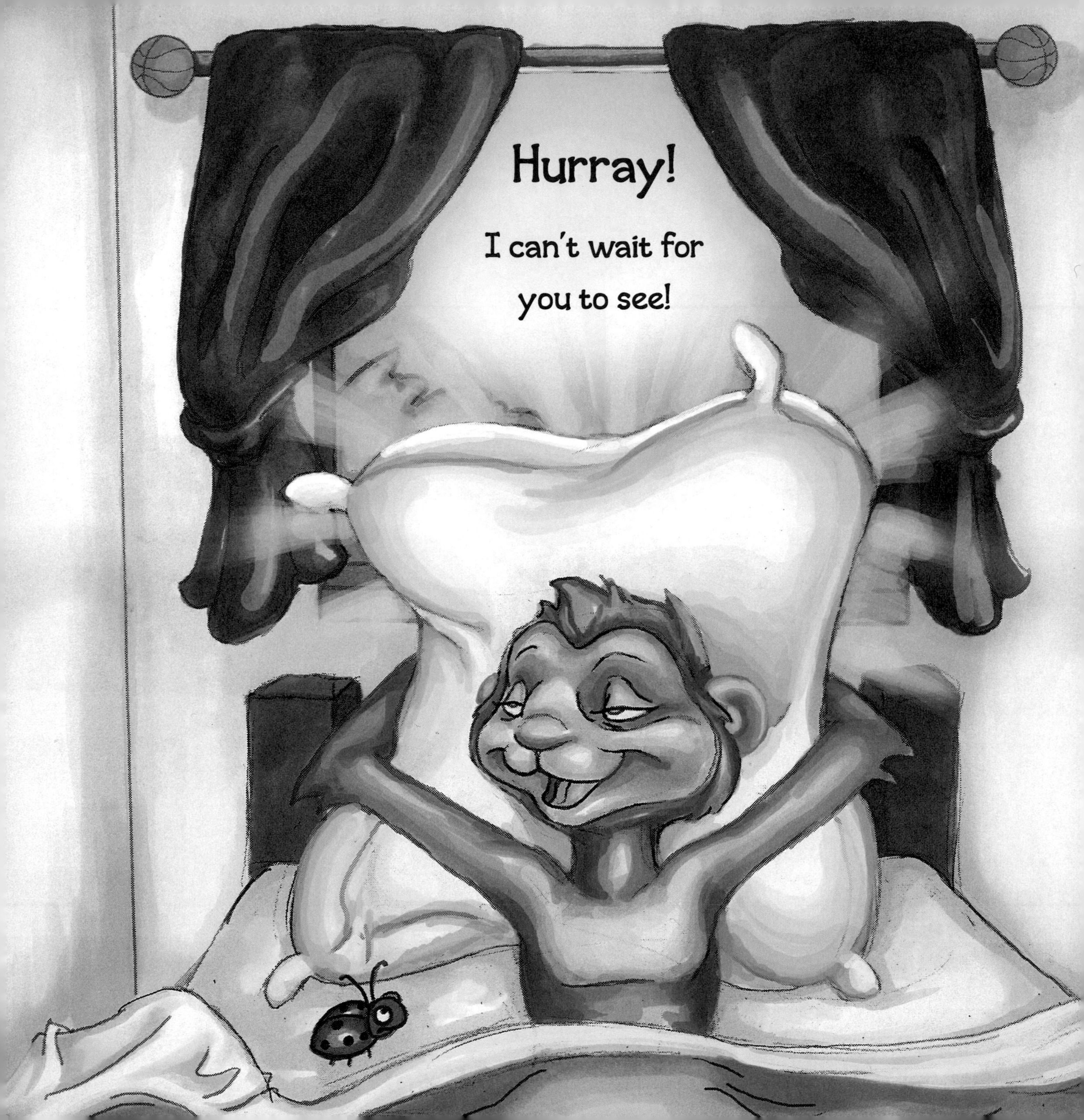

My new big kid pillow.
Just as comfy, soft, and snugly.

This is dedicated to any kid,
old or new.
In memory for your blankie,
woobie, or pillow you outgrew.

I know how it is to miss it so,
as mine, it was so gross,
it had to go.
How much I miss it,
no one will ever know.

But, I admit,
I found a new one,
it's true!
His name is Dave.
I love you.

Color Me In!

Draw a picture of your favorite pillow or blankie here.

About the Illustrator

HOLLIE MENGERT is a recent college graduate with a BFA in media arts and animation. She has loved drawing since she was young and is proud to now call it her career. Her experiences range from various free lance illustration jobs and logo work to a year long internship at Cricket Moon Media. In addition she has done character design work, concept art and animation for several companies and nonprofit organizations. She currently resides in Seattle, Washington, where she enjoys time with family and friends in addition to her many artistic endeavors.
My Pillow and Me is her first illustrated children's book, and she has enjoyed every minute of its development as well as working with Writer Christina Nixon Cole.

About the Author

CHRISTINA NIXON COLE is a new author in children's poetry. She has her degree in art and jewelry design, and teaches glass beadmaking in her home studio in San Diego, California. She's married to her wonderful husband, Dave. They enjoy long days at the beach, visits to Disneyland, and taking their cute Shiba Inu dog named Ryu on walks. Christina is also a Certified Hypnotherapist and EFT coach. She's enjoyed each step of creating her first children's book and hopes to publish more of them in the future. It's been such a fantastic journey working with such a talented Illustrator, Hollie Mengert, who gave this story its true color and life.

www.ladybookpublishing.com